KU-002-965

Bump in The Night

igloobooks

Vampire Storm

It was a grey and rainy evening. Dean and Jenna sat by the small desk in Dean's bedroom. "We've got to think of an idea for the school art competition," said Jenna. "Are you listening, Dean?" It was quite obvious that her brother wasn't. He stared intently out of the window, deep in thought.

Outside, street lamps flickered into life. The day was fading and a cold moon had begun to rise. "I know," said Dean, suddenly, making Jenna jump. "Let's do something scary, like a mutant, cyber-vampire. I'll sketch it and you can finish it on the computer." Jenna smiled. She could always trust her brother's bright ideas.

After much scribbling and rubbing-out, the sketch was ready. Dean had drawn a thin figure with a stooped body and an overly large head. On its face, one eye slanted downwards and the wide mouth sagged in a strange grimace that exposed two sharp, white fangs. Grey eye-bags hung low over hollow cheeks and the picture had the appearance of a tired undertaker.

Jenna scanned the drawing, then she added light and shadow and a dash of red. "That's brought him to life." said Dean.

Suddenly, something banged hard against the bedroom window. They both jumped back in alarm. "It's just the wind," said Dean. "It's really picking up, there'll be a storm tonight, for sure."
Jenna stretched and yawned. "I'm off to bed." she said.

Vampire Storm

Dean reached over to switch the computer off. "Goodnight creepy vampire!" he said. Outside, a bolt of lightning ripped across the sky. The screen buzzed and crackled. Dean pressed the button to shut down the computer, but nothing happened. So, he sloped off to bed, leaving the computer cursor blinking in the dark.

The night crept on. Outside, lightning split the dark. The computer flickered wildly and a pale, green light began to seep from the screen. It spilled out over the desk and down onto the carpet, while outside, thunder crashed and boomed.

Dean woke with a start to see something moving nearby. A familiar figure stood by the window. It was tall with a stooped body and large head. Dean rubbed his eyes and stared in disbelief. The vampire had come alive. "What do you want?" stammered Dean, his heart pounding in his chest.

The figure opened its mouth and said, "Food." Dean flicked on the light. "He's a vampire and he wants food, that means he wants blood!" he cried.

The figure stretched out its arms and moved forward. Frozen with fear, Dean closed his eyes and waited for the first bite, but nothing happened. Instead, there was an odd whooshing noise nearby. When he opened his eyes, he saw that the vampire was draining his bedside lamp of power. The light fizzled, spluttered and then went out.

Dean ran to Jenna's room and switched on the light. "Get up," he said in a hard whisper, "It's come to life."

"What has?" asked Jenna, sleepily. Then she saw it standing in the doorway. Jenna stifled a scream when the lights went out.

"He's draining the power," said Dean. "He wants the electricity."

The vampire turned around and lumbered towards the stairs. "There's loads of electrical stuff downstairs," croaked Dean.

"Yeah, there's the cooker, the fridge and the brand new TV," said Jenna.

They raced after the creature.

Vampire Storm

Downstairs, the vampire crouched near the fridge. There was a 'whooshing' sound and the fridge stopped humming. "Do something," said Jenna,"If we don't stop him, he'll drain the whole house, maybe even the whole neighbourhood!"

Dean looked around. In a panic, he ran to the sink. He grabbed a jug, half-full of water and threw it over the creature. It made a sloshing, splattering sound. There was a short silence, while the confused figure swayed backwards and forwards, as small sparks flew from its body. Suddenly the creature let out a long moan and fell backwards, with a crash, onto the hall table.

Vampire Storm

For a moment, the hallway was deathly quiet. Then, a light flicked on upstairs. "What's going on down there?" said an irritated, sleepy voice. It was Dad. The vampire quickly recovered from his dousing when he noticed the light. "Food," it groaned and lurched towards the stairs.

"We've got to distract him," said Dean desperately.
Outside, a stark bolt of lightning flashed. It lit up the hallway. The vampire turned towards it and Dean had an idea. He fumbled for something in the pocket of a coat, hanging in the hallway. Pulling out a bunch of keys, he shoved one in the door lock and opened it with a click.

Vampire Storm

"Come, on, Vampire," he called, "This way." He flung the door open, just as another bolt of lightning struck. The vampire stumbled out of the door and into the garden. Lightning flashed and thunder boomed. The lashing rain splashed and fizzled on the creature's body. Jenna and Dean watched as it began to judder and fade until nothing was left but a series of small, sputtering sparks.

Dean turned to Jenna. They looked round at the splintered table and then at the strangely quiet fridge in the kitchen. "Dad'll be down the stairs any minute. He'll want an explanation." said Dean.

"We'll put it all down to the storm," said Jenna, "And as for the school art competition, I think we should stick to still life."

The Haunted Halloween

Everything was ready for Alex's Halloween party. The spooky decorations were hung up, the eyeball sweets were in bowls and the pumpkin cakes were baked. All Alex had to do was put on his Frankenstein's monster costume. He was quite looking forward to having a bolt through his neck.

As the guests arrived, Alex's mum showed them in. Alex put some creepy music on the stereo, full of weird screams and howls. Alex's mum brought out trays of cookies shaped like rats and a whole heap of spider-shaped jellies.

Everyone wore weird and wonderful Halloween costumes. However, Alex noticed three children, standing by the food table. One was dressed as a vampire, another as a skeleton in a cape and the third was a ghost in a sheet. There was something strange about their costumes and Alex went to take a closer look.

The vampire had red eyes that looked real. Underneath the skeleton's cape, its bones didn't seem to have anything holding them up. Then Alex looked at the ghost and he could see right through it!

When nobody was looking, Alex walked right up to the ghost and tugged off its sheet. There was nothing underneath. Alex could hardly speak with surprise. "Excuse me," said a little voice, in the space where a body should have been. "Please replace my sheet, I feel invisible without it."
"But you are invisible," whispered Alex, his mouth open wide.

Alex quickly replaced the sheet before anyone noticed. "Please don't be angry with us," said the skeleton, its bones clacking noisily. "We are friendly spooks, honestly."

The Haunted Halloween

"My name is Vertebra," said the skeleton. "The vampire is Vlad and our ghostly friend is Jasper. We came to your party because no one on Hallows End Road, where we live, wants to celebrate Halloween. They all think it's boring."

Alex felt sorry for his new spooky friends. He was sure that, with a little encouragement, their neighbours would join in the Halloween celebrations. Then he had an idea. "My party is nearly over," he said. "Everyone will be going off trick or treating, why don't we go to Hallows End Road?"

"I'm coming with you," insisted Alex's mum, when he told her. "Where is this place, anyway?" she asked, "I've never heard of it."

The Haunted Halloween

Hallows End Road was much nearer to Alex's house then he, or his mum, realised. "I can't imagine why we have never noticed it before," said Mum. She looked around at the misshapen houses that lurked in shadow, under the bright, full moon and she felt strangely uneasy.

It was getting dark when Alex knocked at the door of a ramshackle house. The front door creaked open and a man with a hairy, wolf-like face and clawed hands, stood grinning at them. "Trick or treat," said Alex bravely.
The man growled, threw some cookies at them and slammed the door.

"How rude," said Alex's mum, "but I have to say, that Wolfman costume looked incredibly real." She laughed nervously and the others just looked at each other.

Vertebra examined one of the cookies. "They're dog biscuits," she said, throwing them into a flower bed. "What a nasty trick."

The second house was as big as a castle. It was opened by a hunchbacked man with huge, bulging eyes. "Do you wish to speak to the master?" he said in a creepy, whispery voice.

"Actually, we wanted to know if you'd like a trick or a treat," replied Alex.

Before the hunchback had time to answer, a scary voice boomed out from the grim hall behind. "At last, I have almost brought the monster to life," shrieked the mad voice. There followed a terrible crackling sound and a hideous groaning and moaning.

The hunchback looked frightened. "We must not anger the master," he said and quietly closed the door.

Next, Alex knocked on the door of a horrible cottage. It was opened by a ragged-looking witch. She had long, filthy nails and limp, greasy hair. There was a suspicious sound of bubbling coming from inside the cottage and a terrible smell wafted past.

The witch smiled and cackled, loudly. "Here you go, children," she wheezed, handing them some very weird-looking, black sweets. "This is my finest recipe, black beetles in castor oil. Try them, they're delicious." With that, the witch gave an ear-piercing shriek and shut the door.

Vlad tasted one of the sticky sweets and promptly spat it out. "It tried to bite me back," he said.

"I think I've had enough of Halloween," said Vertebra, "I want to go home."

The Haunted Halloween

She led them to a tall house at the end of the road and knocked on the door. A skeleton appeared, wearing clothes like tramp. "Dad!" cried Vertebra. She ran into the house and hugged the skeleton with a clackety, rattling sound. Vlad and Jasper followed her inside.

Alex's mum went rather pale. "There is something very strange about the people who live around here," she whispered, "I think I'd like to go home, too." Alex, quickly lead his bewildered mother down the garden path.

"Please come and visit us again," pleaded Vertebra.

"Goodbye, Alex," said Vlad and Jasper, "we hope we didn't ruin your party?"

"No," said Alex, "you made this the best haunted Halloween ever."

Blood Spider

It was the evening before school sports day. Ben wasn't looking forward to it. He always came last in the races, thanks to his asthma. It didn't help that Roy Briggs, the fastest runner in the school, laughed at Ben when he was practicing.

"I wish I was stronger and able to run faster," said Ben, as he gasped for breath. He sat at the edge of the sports field and fumbled for his inhaler, but it slipped from his hand and dropped into the long grass. As Ben reached down, a sharp pain shot through his hand.

"Ouch!" cried Ben, sucking his finger, which was throbbing painfully. It was then that he noticed the spider. It was small with a blood-red stripe across its back, it was unlike any species he had ever seen. It scuttled off into the grass before Ben could capture it.

Back in class, the afternoon dragged. Ben forgot about the small bite on his hand until it began to throb again, later in the day. When he looked at it, two small puncture marks were visible and he noticed that the veins around the wound had swollen and ran like thick, purple rivulets towards his fingers. The throbbing in Ben's hand seemed to get worse. It was as if it was spreading slowly, making its way around his body. Ben was worried. "I've got to find out what kind of spider bit me," he thought. "I'll go and see Alice, she'll be able to help."

The school bell rang and Ben dashed outside. He headed towards Alice's house, jogging slowly at first and then going faster and faster, blood pumping furiously through his veins. The roads and traffic seemed like a blur and suddenly, he was standing outside Alice's front door.

Blood Spider

Alice, Ben's best friend, looked in every book she could think of, but there was no such spider anywhere. The only book left was one belonging to her Dad, about myths and legends. Alice scanned it and suddenly let out a surprised gasp. "According to this, you have been bitten by a blood spider!" she said. "They are the stuff of legend. Anyone bitten by this spider can move extremely fast and they're almost unstoppable."

It was getting late. "I've got to go," said Ben. Alice agreed to do some research on the mythical spider and let him know what she found.
Meanwhile, Ben raced home at the speed of light.
Ben went to bed and didn't speak to anyone. His hand was throbbing and even his

Blood Spider

bones seemed to hurt. He looked down and saw that his hands were pulsing, and thick, long nails were growing. "What's happening to me?" asked Ben, as a cold rush of fear swept over him. He switched off the light and dived under the covers. Eventually the wild pulsing lessened and he fell into an uneasy sleep.

Blood Spider

The next day was sports day. Ben felt quite normal as he got changed in the locker room. Then, suddenly, a fly buzzed past. He had to resist a powerful urge to snatch at the fly and stuff it into his mouth. Luckily, the teacher had just called the class outside, the first race was about to begin and Ben was running in it.

On the track, everyone lined up for the race. Roy threw his usual sneering looks at Ben. Then, the starting whistle blew. Ben could feel the spider venom rushing through him. He let Roy take the lead, but, just as the finish line was in sight, Ben shot forward in a burst of spider-speed. Roy was astonished to see him hurtle past and win the gold medal.

Blood Spider

After the race, Alice ran up to him. "I did some more research," she panted. "The spider venom only stays in the body until the full moon and that's tonight. However, the symptoms might get worse, before they get better." she warned.

Ben was relieved that he wasn't going to be a spider-freak forever. He changed into his normal clothes and smiled at the thought of Roy's fury at losing the race. Then Ben looked in the mirror and his blood ran cold.

His eyes had turned bright red. "I hope Alice is right about this wearing off by tonight." he thought, suddenly worried. Ben pulled his sweatshirt hood over his head and made his way home, hoping he wouldn't see anyone.

Walking down the last street that led to his house, Ben heard someone coming up behind him. Without warning, he was shoved roughly into a shadowy area under a clump of trees. Then a familiar voice spoke.

"Hey, freak," hissed Roy Briggs, "How did you win that race? No one can run faster than me."

Ben felt the venom tingle as it rushed through his veins. "But I did run faster," he said, "So, you'd better watch out."

Roy looked Ben up and down and burst out laughing. "I'm not scared of a weakling like you!" he said, maliciously.